The Pumpkin Elf Mystery

by ABBY KLEIN

illustrated by
JOHN MCKINLEY

THE BLUE SKY PRESS
An Imprint of Scholastic Inc. • New York

To children everywhere who believe
in the Pumpkin Elf's magic.
Happy Halloween!
A. K.

THE BLUE SKY PRESS

Text copyright © 2007 by Abby Klein
Illustrations copyright © 2007 by John McKinley
All rights reserved.

Special thanks to Robert Martin Staenberg.

Library of Congress catalog card number 2006025858.
ISBN 10: 0-439-89591-X / ISBN 13: 978-0-439-89591-0
10 9 8 7 6 5 4   07 08 09 10 11
Printed in the United States of America   40
First printing, August 2007

CHAPTERS

I have a problem.

A really, really, big problem.

My class is having a

pumpkin-decorating contest,

but my pumpkin

has disappeared!

Let me tell you about it.

CHAPTER 1

A Clue

"A clue! A clue! I think I found a clue!" Max was yelling and waving something around in the air as I walked into the classroom.

"What's he saying?" I asked my best friend, Robbie.

"I don't know," Robbie said, shrugging his shoulders. "Something about a clue."

"Let me see! Let me see!" Chloe squealed, trying to grab whatever was in Max's hand.

"Hey, keep your dirty little paws off!" Max said, pushing Chloe's hand out of the way.

"Mrs. Wushy," Chloe whined, "Max won't let me see what's in his hand! That's not fair. It's not his."

"You're right," said our teacher, Mrs. Wushy. "The Pumpkin Elf left that clue for the whole class. May I have it, please, Max?"

"Did she just say the 'Pumpkin Elf'?"

"It sure sounded like it, but I have no idea what she's talking about!" said Jessie.

"Me neither," whispered Robbie. "I think Mrs. Wushy's going crazy."

"Boys and girls, please come to the rug. I have something very special to share with all of you."

Everybody came quickly to sit on the rug. We were all so curious about the piece of paper Mrs. Wushy was holding in her hand.

"This pumpkin-shaped piece of paper is a very special clue."

"I saw it first!" Max yelled, jumping up from his spot on the rug.

Chloe popped up and stuck her finger in Max's face. "That's only because you pulled it off the wall before anybody else could even see it, you big meanie!"

"Did not!"

"Did too!"

"Chloe. Max. Both of you need to sit down and be quiet. I can't read this special message until everyone is ready to listen. I would like you two to sit on opposite sides of the rug."

When they were finally seated, Mrs. Wushy continued. "As I was saying, this pumpkin-shaped piece of paper is a clue from the Pumpkin Elf."

Jessie raised her hand.

"Yes, Jessie."

"Did you just say the 'Pumpkin Elf'?"

"Yes, I did," Mrs. Wushy said, smiling.

"I've heard of Santa Claus and the Easter Bunny, but I've never heard of the Pumpkin Elf."

"Then you're in for a real treat," said Mrs. Wushy.

"Who is the Pumpkin Elf?" asked Robbie.

"The Pumpkin Elf is a little elf with a pumpkin-shaped head who comes around at Halloween time to play tricks and leave treats for kids."

"Cool," said Max. "When do we get to see this guy?"

"He's very hard to see," said Mrs. Wushy. "He's small, and he can run very fast."

"Have you ever seen him?" I asked.

"One morning when I was unlocking the classroom door, I saw a blur of something orange run between my legs. I am pretty sure it was him."

"What was he doing?"

"Playing tricks! He had made a big mess in the classroom."

"What did he do?" asked Robbie.

"He had thrown the orange crayons all over the floor and pulled all the orange blocks off the shelf. He even left orange footprints all over the place!"

"No way!" we all gasped.

"He's a very sneaky little fellow."

"What's the clue for?" asked Jessie.

"Remember that I said he also likes to give treats? He usually leaves us clues so we can find some treats he's left for us."

"Read the clue! Read the clue!" Chloe squealed, clapping her hands.

Everyone in the class joined in, chanting, "Read the clue! Read the clue!"

Mrs. Wushy put her finger to her lips. "All of you need to be very quiet if you want me to read the clue," she whispered.

The whole room went silent. We stared at Mrs. Wushy. She cleared her throat. "Ahem . . . the clue says:

I am the Pumpkin Elf, and I'm here to say
that tomorrow might be your lucky day!
Listen to your teacher
and your mom and dad, too,
and I just might leave something
special for you!

"Our lucky day!" Max repeated. "All right!" Then he turned to me with his hand in the air. "High five, Freddy."

I gave Max a high five. Wow! That Pumpkin Elf must really have some kind of magic powers if he can make Max, the biggest bully in the whole first grade, nice for even a minute.

"What's the special something he leaves for us?" asked Chloe. "I just love surprises!"

"Well, it wouldn't be much of a surprise if

I told you, now would it?" said Mrs. Wushy. "Besides, I don't know any more than you. We'll all just have to wait until tomorrow."

"Awwww," the class moaned together.

"But remember—the clue says you have to be good and listen to your teacher and your mom and dad. If you don't behave, then he won't come."

"Did you hear that, Max?" Chloe yelled across the rug. "You'd better not spoil it for the rest of us!"

"Be quiet, you little prissy princess," said Max. "You're the one who's going to spoil it!"

"Max. Chloe. You two need to be on your very best behavior, or he won't come back," said Mrs. Wushy.

"Great!" I whispered to Robbie. "He's never going to come with those two around."

"Don't worry, Freddy. He'll come."

"How do you know?"

"I just have a good feeling about this."

"Me too," I said, smiling. "I can't wait!"

CHAPTER 2

Have You Seen the Pumpkin Elf?

"Guess who came to our class today?" I said excitedly, as we sat down to dinner.

"Let me guess," said my mom. "Mr. Pendergast."

"The principal? No!"

"Miss Betsy?"

"The music teacher? It's not music day. Why would she come to our class?"

"Sorry. I thought she came on Tuesdays."

"It wasn't anybody from school."

"Oh, I know who it is," said my dad, smiling and nodding.

"You do?"

"Yes, it was Officer Bill, the policeman."

"I love him!" my sister, Suzie, added.

"Ughhh, no!" I sighed. "It was not Mr. Pendergast, or Miss Betsy, or Officer Bill. Do you give up?"

"Yes, we give up," said my mom. "Tell us."

"The Pumpkin Elf!"

"The who?"

"The Pumpkin Elf!"

"No way!" said Suzie. "You are so lucky."

"Would one of you mind telling me and your mother who the Pumpkin Elf is?"

"Don't you remember?" said Suzie. "When I was in Mrs. Wushy's class, the Pumpkin Elf came and played tricks and left us treats."

"Oh yes," said my mom. "I remember now."

"Mrs. Wushy said that he looks like a little elf with a pumpkin-shaped head. Have you ever seen him, Mom?"

"No, I haven't, sweetie."

"That's probably because he is so fast," said Suzie. "He doesn't want to get caught."

"That's what Mrs. Wushy said. She said she thought she saw him once, but he's so fast that she didn't really get a good look at him."

"Did he leave you any clues?" asked Suzie.

"Yeah, he left one that said he might come
back tomorrow with some treats."

"Might?" said my mom.

"He only comes if you are good. The clue
said that we had to listen to our teacher and
our mom and dad."

"Is that so?" said my dad, chuckling.

"When I was in Mrs. Wushy's class, he left us a whole bunch of clues that we had to follow. He took us on a hunt all over the school."

"I'm so excited I can hardly wait!" I said, bouncing in my seat.

"Freddy, calm down," said my mom. "You're going to spill your macaroni all over the floor."

"Sorry, Mom."

"How about if you do a little more eating and a little less talking? You haven't even touched your food."

"Did you ever see him, Suzie?" I asked, shoveling macaroni into my mouth.

"Freddy, it's not polite to talk with your mouth full," said my mom.

I nodded, smiled, gave her the thumbs-up, and swallowed what was in my mouth.

"I saw something small and orange run past me on the playground, but I couldn't catch him," said Suzie.

I shoved more macaroni into my mouth. "I really want to catch him."

"Freddy, what did your mother say about talking with your mouth full? Aren't you supposed to be listening to your parents if you want the Pumpkin Elf to come?"

I looked at my dad and gulped. "Right-o! Sorry, Dad. I won't do it again."

"Wear your orange T-shirt to school

tomorrow," said Suzie. "The Pumpkin Elf's favorite color is orange."

"Really? What else does he like?"

"He likes to give out pumpkins and treats around Halloween."

"Cool."

"Freddy, if you're done eating, then it's time to take a bath."

"Awww, Mom. Do I have to?"

"Remember, the Pumpkin Elf is watching. You wouldn't want to disappoint him."

"Oh yeah, right. I'm on my way to the bathroom now!" I said as I jumped up and started running out of the kitchen.

"Don't forget to wash behind your ears!" my mom called after me.

"I won't!" I called back.

As I started to climb the stairs, I thought I saw a flash of orange at the top of the staircase. Could it be . . . ? I ran to the top of the stairs, but nothing was there.

CHAPTER 3

Tricks or Treats

The next morning, as soon as I got off the bus, I ran to my classroom. I couldn't wait to see if the Pumpkin Elf had come overnight. The classroom door was locked, but all of the kids were looking in the window and jumping up and down, yelling, "He came! He came!"

I tried to squeeze my way in to get a good look, but Max shoved me back with a hard elbow to the stomach. "Hey! I'm standing here. Go find your own spot!"

I was so excited about the Pumpkin Elf that

not even Max could ruin my day. I held my stomach and pushed through a bunch of kids one more time. Finally, I got right up against the window. Then a familiar voice whispered in my ear, "Can you believe what he did?"

I would know that voice anywhere. It was Jessie. I turned to her. "What? What did the Pumpkin Elf do? I just got here, and I didn't get to see anything yet."

"He made a mess of the classroom! Just like Mrs. Wushy said. He threw the orange crayons all over the place, cut up pieces of orange paper and left scraps everywhere, and the orange blocks are all over the floor!"

I peered into the window. I was shocked. "No way! What a mess! How did he get into the room if it was locked?"

Just then Mrs. Wushy walked up. "Hello, everybody. What's all the commotion about?"

"The Pumpkin Elf! The Pumpkin Elf was here!" we all yelled.

"What are you talking about?"

"The Pumpkin Elf came," said Max.

"He did?" said Mrs. Wushy. "But the door was locked while I was up at the office. I wonder how he got in?"

"Hey, I was wondering that, too, Mrs. Wushy," I said.

"Maybe he can change his molecular structure so he can fit into unusually small spaces," said Robbie.

Robbie is my best friend, and he is a science genius. He knows everything about everything.

"Whatever, Brainiac," said Max.

"I think he has magic powers," said Chloe. "Just like fairies. I bet he can make himself invisible and float through walls."

"Maybe he comes down the chimney like Santa Claus," said Max.

"The chimney?" I whispered to Robbie.

"The chimney? You're crazy," said Jessie. "There aren't any chimneys at school!" Leave it to Jessie to have the guts to tell Max what I was only thinking.

Mrs. Wushy unlocked the door, and we all stumbled over one another, trying to be the first one in the room. We ran around, looking at the huge mess that tricky little elf had made. We knew he did it because there were little orange footprints all over the place.

"I know the Pumpkin Elf was here because of these little orange footprints," said Max.

"I think he should be a detective when he grows up," Robbie whispered to me.

"Yeah. He's a genius. I don't know how he figured that out!" We both burst out laughing.

"Just look at this mess!" said Mrs. Wushy. "That Pumpkin Elf is so naughty!"

"Who's going to clean it up?" Chloe asked, wrinkling her nose.

Who did she think? The maid?

"You! You're going to clean it up, fancy-pants," said Max.

"Me? But that's not fair! I just got my nails painted orange yesterday for this special occasion. I don't want to chip one."

"You're not going to do it by yourself, Chloe. Everyone is going to help," said Mrs. Wushy. She turned to the class. "Okay, everybody. Let's start getting this mess picked up."

We zoomed all over the room, picking up crayons, blocks, and little scraps of paper.

"Do you think he's watching us right now?" I asked Jessie.

"Oh yeah. I think he's watching all right, and I think he's laughing at all of us. He thinks it's funny that we are picking up *his* mess."

I quickly glanced around the room, but I didn't see him anywhere.

"As soon as everything is put away, please come to the rug," said Mrs. Wushy. "I want to get started on our morning work."

"Morning work?" groaned Max. "What happened to the treats?"

"What treats?"

"You said that the Pumpkin Elf plays tricks and leaves us treats," said Chloe, with her hands on her hips. "We saw the tricks. Where are the treats?"

"Do I look like a Pumpkin Elf?" said Mrs. Wushy. "I don't know anything about treats."

"But you *said*," Max complained.

"I said that he plays tricks and sometimes leaves treats. I think his clue yesterday said that he *might* leave treats but only if you were good listeners."

"Awww . . . " moaned Max.

"Max, stop complaining, or we might not get any treats," said Jessie.

"Jessie's right," said Mrs. Wushy. "If I were you, Max, I would be on my best behavior."

"Oh, fine," Max sighed, crossing his arms, "but he'd better come soon."

"Boys and girls, today we are going to learn about telling time."

"I know what time it is!" Max interrupted. "It's time for the Pumpkin Elf to leave us those treats!"

"Max," said Mrs. Wushy, "one more word out of you, and you're going straight to Mr. Pendergast's office. If I have to send you there, then you might miss the treats. This is your last chance. Do you understand?"

Max nodded his head and pretended to zip his lips closed.

Nobody, not even Max, wanted to miss the treats . . . that is, if there were any treats. I was starting to wonder.

It was then that I saw it . . . a little piece of orange paper sticking out from behind the October sign on the calendar.

CHAPTER 4

The Hunt

"Um, excuse me, Mrs. Wushy, but what is that?"

"What is what, Freddy?"

"That little piece of orange paper sticking out from behind the October sign," I said, pointing to the calendar.

"I don't know. Let me see."

Mrs. Wushy pulled out the piece of orange paper shaped like a pumpkin, and we all started chanting, "It's a clue! It's a clue!"

"Well, you all are right. It does look like another clue from the Pumpkin Elf."

"Read it! Read it!" we all yelled.

"If everyone will be quiet, I'll tell you what it says."

A hush fell over the room. "It says:

> If you want to find my treats,
> then you must be quick on your feet.
> Follow my clues, one by one,
> and you just might find a surprise
> before the day is done.

We all jumped to our feet and started clapping. "Let's go! Let's go!"

"Hold on a minute, boys and girls. This elf is a tricky little fellow. How do we know he's not just trying to fool us?"

"He wouldn't do that," said Chloe.

"Let's go! Let's go!" we all chanted again.

"Well, okay," said Mrs. Wushy, "but I don't know if this is the best idea. He might just be playing a trick on us.

"Let's see what the rest of the clue says," said Mrs. Wushy. She started to read:

Step outside, and do as I say.
Go to the place where you all like to play.

"Where is that?"

"The playground! The playground! He left us treats on the playground!"

We all ran to line up at the door.

"Follow me in a straight line, boys and girls. We'll go look on the playground."

When we got to the playground, we all spread out to look for the treats. We looked on the slide, under the monkey bars, and in the playhouse, but we didn't find any treats.

"I told you he was tricky," said Mrs. Wushy.

"Hey, I think I found another clue," Robbie called as he ran up, holding another pumpkin-shaped piece of paper in his hand.

"What does it say?"

Mrs. Wushy read the next clue:

I got hungry,
so I moved the treats.
I took them to the place
where you all go to eat.

"The cafeteria! The cafeteria! He took the treats to the cafeteria!"

We walked over to the cafeteria, but the only thing we found there was the lunch lady, who was setting up for lunch.

"Did you see the Pumpkin Elf around here?" we asked her.

"As a matter of fact, he just ran by a few minutes ago. He grabbed a hot dog, but when he saw me, he took off like a bolt of lightning. He dropped this, though," she said, pulling an orange piece of paper out of her pocket. "I have no idea what it is."

"Another clue! Another clue! Read it, Mrs. Wushy! Read it!"

A door was open, so I ran in to look.
I found myself in a room full of books.

"The library! The library! He moved the treats to the library!"

When we got to the door of the library, Mrs. Wushy stopped. "Remember, boys and girls, the library is a quiet place. No yelling. Please use your inside voices." She opened the door, and we all went in.

We tiptoed around, but there was still no Pumpkin Elf in sight. I was beginning to think that all this was one big trick.

"I don't think there are any treats," I whispered to Robbie.

"Why do you say that?"

"Because we've already been to three places, and he's not at any of them."

"So what are you saying? Do you want to give up, Freddy?"

"No, I guess not."

"Then keep looking!"

Just then, Mrs. Topham, the librarian, came out of her office in the back of the library. "What is going on in here?" she asked.

"We're looking for the Pumpkin Elf. Have you seen him?"

"The who?"

"The Pumpkin Elf. He's small, and he has a head shaped like a pumpkin."

"Oh my goodness! He sounds like quite a character. I'm so sorry, but I haven't seen him. I did find this on the checkout counter," said Mrs. Topham, handing Mrs. Wushy a pumpkin-shaped piece of paper.

"Not another clue!" groaned Max. "I don't want another clue. I want the treats!"

"Let's go back to the room and do math," suggested Mrs. Wushy.

"Noooo!" we all said together. "No math. Read the next clue!"

"All right. It says:

I got tired and thirsty
and needed a drink,
so I went to the place
with toilets and a sink.

"The bathroom!" Max said, laughing. "The Pumpkin Elf went to the bathroom! Ha-ha!"

"Inside voice, Max. Inside voice," said Mrs. Wushy, putting her finger to her lips.

We tiptoed out of the library and walked over to the boys' bathroom.

"Ewww, why are we going to the boys' bathroom?" said Chloe. "Why can't we go to the girls'?"

"Because the Pumpkin Elf is a boy, Ding-Dong," said Max. "He's not allowed in the girls' bathroom."

"Hmph." Chloe pouted, folding her hands across her chest.

"Freddy, would you go into the bathroom and see if the Pumpkin Elf is there?" asked Mrs. Wushy. "The rest of us will wait outside."

My heart started beating faster. I was so excited, I could feel it pounding in my chest. I threw open the bathroom door and ran inside, but the bathroom was empty. There was nothing there. I checked each stall. Still nothing. No Pumpkin Elf. Not even a clue. I walked back out with my head hanging. "There's nothing there," I said softly.

"What do you mean, nothing there?" Max

demanded. "Let me see," he said, shoving me out of the way and running into the bathroom. He came out a few seconds later. "Freddy's right. There's nothing there."

"Awwww," we all moaned.

"Well, it looks like this year there are no treats, only tricks," said Mrs. Wushy. "I warned you all. Let's go back to the classroom."

"No! No! Read the next clue," said Chloe.

"I'm sorry, Chloe. There are no more clues."

We all walked slowly back to our room with our heads hanging, dragging our feet.

"What a bummer," said Jessie.

"I know. I don't think I like this Pumpkin Elf very much."

"Me either," said Robbie.

As we approached the classroom, we saw a note taped to the door.

"What's this?" said Mrs. Wushy. She pulled off the note and started to read:

Now this is a sight I don't like to see:
All these sad faces looking at me.
I played a little trick, that's true,
but now I want to make it up to you.
When you go into the room,
keep your eyes open wide.
I left you a surprise inside.

Mrs. Wushy opened the door, and my eyes almost popped out of my head. I couldn't believe what I saw!

CHAPTER 5

Surprise!

Pumpkins, pumpkins everywhere! The whole room was full of pumpkins!

"Whoa, this is soooooo cool," said Max.

"It looks like a pumpkin patch in here," I said, as my mouth dropped open.

"The Pumpkin Elf really is magic," Jessie whispered to me.

"Boys and girls," said Mrs. Wushy, "it looks as if he left one more clue. I just found it stuck on my chair."

"What does it say? What does it say?"

"It says:

While it was me you were trying to catch,
I set up your room like a pumpkin patch.
There are twenty-one pumpkins:
one for each of you,
and an extra for your teacher, too!
You can decorate them and have lots of fun.
Have a Happy Halloween—I'm on the run!

"Wow!" said Jessie. "Do we really get to have our own pumpkin?"

"Looks like it," said Mrs. Wushy, smiling.

"I have a lot of pumpkins at my house already," Chloe complained.

"But you don't have one from the Pumpkin Elf," I said.

"So?"

"So these are really special."

"They are? What makes them so special?"

"The Pumpkin Elf grew them himself. They are perfect pumpkins!" I said, picking up a pumpkin and running my hands all over it.

"They sure are perfect," said Robbie, inspecting another pumpkin. "He must use special seeds."

"Everyone may choose one pumpkin and bring it to me, so I can write your name on it," said Mrs. Wushy. "Once I have written your name, then please sit down on the rug."

All the kids went to choose a pumpkin.

"Hey, give me that! It's mine!" Max yelled, trying to pull a pumpkin out of Chloe's hands.

"It is not!" Chloe screamed. "I had it first."

"No, I did!"

"I did!"

"No, I did!"

Their tug-of-war with the pumpkin went on for about a minute until Max finally yanked the pumpkin free from Chloe's hands and sent her sailing to the floor. She landed with a loud thump.

"Owww! Owww! Did you see what he just did, Mrs. Wushy?" she wailed. "That was *my* pumpkin."

"What I saw," said Mrs. Wushy, "were two children fighting over a special treat. I don't think the Pumpkin Elf would be very happy to see the two of you behaving like this."

"But . . . but . . . " Chloe sniffled.

"I think you both should apologize, and then you need to pick another pumpkin. Neither of you is going to get this one."

Max and Chloe stared at each other.

"I'm waiting. . . . " said Mrs. Wushy.

"Fine. I'm sorry," Chloe snapped.

"Sorry," Max mumbled.

"Now the two of you need to go choose another pumpkin, and then join the rest of us on the rug."

"But there are only two pumpkins left," Chloe whined.

Could she say anything without whining?

"Well, that's what happens when you and Max spend your time fighting instead of appreciating things that are given to you."

When everyone was finally on the rug, Mrs.

Wushy said, "I have a special announcement to make. We are going to have a contest."

"Oh, I love contests," I whispered to Jessie.

"Me too," she said.

"Our class is going to have a pumpkin-decorating contest."

"Yeah!" we all cheered.

"Today is Wednesday. You are going to take

your pumpkins home, and you will have two days to decorate them any way you like. Then on Friday, you will bring them back, and we will have a contest to see whose is the best."

"Can we do anything we want to them?" Jessie asked.

"Yes," said Mrs. Wushy. "You can carve them, paint them, and even put clothes on them. Be creative and use your imagination."

"Are you going to give a prize to the winner?" Robbie asked.

"Yes. There will be a first-, second-, and third-place winner, and each will receive a prize."

"Prizes, prizes! We love prizes!" we all yelled.

"Good luck, everybody, and remember to be creative. You want yours to be different from everybody else's."

"Mine has to be different," I thought. "Really different! It's got to be like nothing they've ever seen. What am I going to do?" I hit my forehead with the palm of my hand. "Think, think, think!"

CHAPTER 6

The Pumpkin Mystery

"Mom! I'm home!" I called as I opened the front door. "I have some really great news to tell you!"

"Just a sec, honey. I'll be right there!" she called back. "I'm finishing some work on the computer."

I walked into the kitchen and put my pumpkin down on the table. Just then my mom came in. "Freddy, what's that?" she said, pointing to the pumpkin.

"It's a pumpkin, Mom."

"I know what it is, silly. I mean, where did you get it?"

"From the Pumpkin Elf."

"The who?"

"The Pumpkin Elf. He left us clues today, and we went all over school, looking for him. We never found him, but he left piles of pumpkins in our classroom. It was so cool. The whole room looked like a pumpkin patch!"

"That sounds like a lot of fun."

"It was! The Pumpkin Elf left a pumpkin for everyone in the class."

"He sounds like a very generous elf."

"We all got to take our pumpkins home today because we are having a pumpkin-decorating contest. We get to decorate the pumpkins any way we want, and then we bring them back to school on Friday. There are going to be three winners, and they all get prizes! Doesn't that sound cool?"

"Yes, it does, sweetie."

"Will you help me decorate mine, Mom? I want it to be extra special."

"Sure, honey. What did you have in mind?"

"That's the problem. I don't really know."

"Well, let's see. You like baseball. How about making it into a baseball player? We could carve a face, put a baseball cap on the top, and make two little hands out of cardboard that are holding a bat and a ball."

"Nah. Other kids might do a sports one. I want mine to be really different."

"How about a ghost? We could cover the pumpkin with a sheet and draw a scary face on the front of it."

"Ha-ha. A ghost. That's a good one, Mom, but I'm still worried that someone else might think of that, too."

"I'm running out of ideas, honey."

"Running out of ideas for what?" Suzie asked as she walked into the kitchen. She had just come home from school.

"Oh, hi, honey. We were just trying to think of a way for Freddy to decorate this pumpkin."

"Did the Pumpkin Elf leave you clues today?" said Suzie.

"Yep. We looked for him all over school."

"I remember doing that when I was in Mrs. Wushy's class. It was so much fun!"

"I know! And the Pumpkin Elf left everyone a pumpkin."

"Are you going to have the pumpkin-decorating contest?"

"Yeah. But I don't know what to do with mine. I can't think of anything."

Just then the phone rang. My mom jumped up to answer it. "I'll be right back."

I turned to Suzie. "Have any good ideas?"

"What's it worth to you?" she asked, with a big smirk on her face.

"What do you mean?"

"I mean I have a great idea that will win first place, but I'll only tell you if you do my chores for two weeks," she said, holding up her finger for a pinkie swear.

"Two weeks?!"

"Do we have a deal or not?"

"I don't know. Two weeks is a long time."

"It's the best idea ever."

"Fine," I said as we locked pinkies. "It's a deal, but I better win first place. What's this great idea of yours?"

"You like sharks, right?"

"Right."

"You decorate your pumpkin to look like a great white shark."

"A shark? That's a terrific idea," my mom said as she walked back into the room. "Did you think of that, Suzie?"

"Yes, I did," she said, grinning from ear to ear. "I'm full of great ideas."

"You are so sweet to help your brother out like that."

"I know."

"Yeah, really sweet," I muttered under my breath.

"So, Suzie. How do you think we should make it?" asked my mom.

"I thought Freddy could carve a face with a big, scary mouth full of teeth. He could make slits on each side for gills. Then he could cut a fin and a tail out of cardboard and stick one on the top and one on the back."

"That does sound really cool," I said. "Will you help me with it?"

"Sure."

Suzie, my mom, and I worked for a long time. I drew a mouth with lots of sharp teeth and some mean-looking eyes. Then my mom helped me carve it. She also helped me cut the gills. She didn't want me to use a knife by myself. Then I drew a big fin and a tail on some cardboard, and Suzie helped me cut them out. It was hard for me to cut through the cardboard with my little scissors, so Suzie cut with the bigger scissors that she's allowed

to use. We stuck the fin on the top of the
pumpkin and the tail on the back and admired
our masterpiece. My mom even took a picture.

"That looks so cool!" I said.

"You are definitely going to win first prize,"
said Suzie. "I just know it."

"I hope so!"

"It is very creative," said my mom. "I'll be surprised if anyone comes up with a better idea. This is so original."

"Thank you so much," I said, giving them both a hug. "You're the best."

"Now, Freddy," said my mom, "why don't you go put it on the front porch? I need to clean up the kitchen and start making dinner."

"But I don't want anything to happen to it, Mom. It's a very special pumpkin. I'll just go put it in my room."

"I don't want it in your room. It's dirty, and it will attract all kinds of bugs. Don't worry. Nothing's going to happen to it out on the porch. Besides, if you leave it there, the whole neighborhood can see your beautiful work before you have to take it to school."

"Oh, all right," I said, and I lifted it off the table and started toward the front door.

"I'll open the door for you," Suzie said, and she ran up behind me.

"Thanks."

She opened the door, and I carefully set the pumpkin down on the front porch. "It is really cool," I said. "I hope it's a winner."

"I know it's a winner," said Suzie.

We closed the door and went back inside to

start our homework. After a little while, I heard my dad's car in the driveway. "Dad's home! Dad's home!" I yelled, jumping up and down.

"Calm down, dork," said Suzie. "Why are you acting so crazy?"

"I can't wait to hear what Dad has to say about the pumpkin."

My dad walked into the room, but the only thing he said was, "Hi, everybody. How was your day?"

"That's it?" I said.

"What do you mean, 'That's it'?"

"That's all you have to say?"

"Freddy, what are you talking about? What do you want me to say?"

"How about 'Who made that really cool pumpkin out there on the porch?' or 'Wow! That shark pumpkin is awesome!'"

"Would someone like to help me out here?" said my dad. "I have no idea what Freddy is talking about. Suzie, do you know what he's talking about?"

"Yes, Dad. He carved a pumpkin to look like a shark for his class contest. It's sitting out on the front porch. Didn't you see it when you came in?"

"No."

"What do you mean, *no*?" I said. "You have to practically walk over it to get in the house. You can't miss it."

"I'm telling you, I didn't see a pumpkin on the front porch."

"Ugh! Dad, stop teasing me."

"I'm not teasing you, Freddy. There is no pumpkin out front."

"Fine. Fine. Come with me, and I'll show it to you."

My dad followed me to the front of the house. I threw open the door.

"Ta-da! Right there," I said, pointing in the direction of the pumpkin. "The first-place pumpkin is right . . . " I stopped mid-sentence. My eyes flew wide open, and my jaw dropped.

My pumpkin was gone!

CHAPTER 7

More Clues

"It's gone! It's gone! My pumpkin is gone! Somebody stole my pumpkin!" I cried.

"Calm down, Freddy," said my dad. "No one stole your pumpkin."

"Where is it, then? It didn't swim away!"

My mom came running out. "What's all the noise about? I thought I heard someone crying. Did someone get hurt?"

"My pumpkin . . . is . . . somebody . . . stole . . . pumpkin!" I said between sobs.

"What are you saying, Freddy? I can't understand you when you're crying," said my mom. "Take a few deep breaths, and then try telling me again."

"Oh, I'll just tell you," said Suzie. "The pumpkin isn't here, Mom. Something happened to it."

"Oh dear."

"Now everybody's getting upset for nothing," said my dad. "Don't worry. We'll find it."

"How? How are we going to find it? I think we should call the police."

"The police! That's a good one," Suzie said, laughing. "The police do not go looking for missing pumpkins."

"We don't need the police," said my dad. "We'll be detectives. We'll look for clues. Freddy, you and Mom go down the street that way, and Suzie and I will go this way. Everybody keep your eyes open for anything suspicious. Good luck!"

My mom grabbed my hand. "Come on, Freddy. Let's go find that pumpkin."

We started to walk down the street. "What kind of clues are we looking for, Mom?"

"Oh, I don't know . . . a footprint . . . a piece of cardboard . . . maybe even a piece of the pumpkin."

"A piece of pumpkin! Don't say that! That would mean that the pumpkin was ruined!"

"Maybe a kid in the neighborhood borrowed it because he wanted to make one just like it."

"But if you don't ask first, then that's stealing. Right, Mom?"

"You're right. The person should have asked first. We would have been happy to let him borrow it for a little while."

We walked, and walked, and walked. "We're never going to find my pumpkin!" I moaned. "We've been walking forever, and we haven't even found one clue!"

"Don't worry, honey, we'll find it."

"No we won't. It's gone, and now I can't enter the contest!"

As we walked past Mrs. Golden's house, she

and her dog, Baxter, were sitting outside on the front porch.

"Why, Freddy, and Mrs. Thresher, what a nice surprise," said Mrs. Golden. "Are you out for a little walk this evening?"

"Actually," I said, "we're looking for something that was stolen from my house."

"Stolen! Oh my goodness! That's terrible," said Mrs. Golden. "What was stolen?"

"A pumpkin I decorated for a class contest."

"Now why would anyone want to steal your pumpkin?"

"That's what I'd like to know," I said.

"Well, is there any way that I can help?"

"I doubt it," I mumbled.

"Freddy," said my mom, "Mrs. Golden is being very sweet. You don't need to be rude to her. Please apologize."

"Sorry, Mrs. Golden. I'm just really sad that someone stole my pumpkin. My mom and sister and I worked so hard on it."

"Oh, believe me, I understand, Freddy. I wish there was some way I could help."

Just then, Baxter barked and came running over to me.

"Oh look," said Mrs. Golden. "Baxter wants to help, too."

"What is it, boy?" I asked. "Did you see the bad guy who stole my pumpkin? Who is it?" He wagged his tail. "Tell me who did it."

I bent down to pet him as I always do, and something poked me in the knee. "Owww!" I cried, rubbing my knee.

"What happened, Freddy?" asked Mrs. Golden. "Are you okay?"

"Something just poked me in the knee." I sat back and looked at the ground. "Here it is," I said, holding up a piece of something small.

"What is it?"

I turned it over in my hand.

"I'm not sure."

"Let me see it, honey," said my mom.

I gave her the piece, and she stared at it for a long time, turning it over and over in her hand. "Hmm," she said.

"Hmm, what?"

"This looks like a piece of pumpkin to me."

"That's strange," said Mrs. Golden. "I haven't bought any pumpkins yet this year. I wonder how that could have landed on my porch? Now we have two mysteries."

I scratched my head. "Something bizarre is definitely going on here," I said. Baxter came over and licked my face. His breath smelled kind of funny. I sniffed Baxter's fur. "Hey, Mom, come smell Baxter. His fur smells weird."

"I'd rather not, honey. You know how I feel about dogs." She turned to Baxter. "Nothing personal, Baxter."

Baxter barked again and wagged his tail.

"I'll smell him," said Mrs. Golden. "Come here, Baxter," she called. "Let me smell you, baby. What did you get into?"

Baxter ran over to her. She took a big whiff of his fur. "Why, I'd know that smell anywhere," said Mrs. Golden. "He smells like a pumpkin!"

"That's exactly what he smells like!" I said.

"But why?"

"Yeah, why?"

I hit my forehead with the palm of my hand. "Think, think, think," I muttered under my breath. All of a sudden, I sat up straight. "I think *I* know why," I said. "I think Baxter *ate* my pumpkin."

"What?" said Mrs. Golden.

"What?" said my mom. "That's ridiculous, Freddy. Dogs don't eat pumpkins."

I walked over to Baxter and pried open his mouth. I wasn't afraid to do it, because Baxter knows me really, really well. His teeth were full of pumpkin pulp. "Well, *this* dog does," I said. "And he's not very good at hiding the evidence. He's got little pieces of pumpkin stuck in his teeth."

"Oh no, Freddy," said Mrs. Golden. "I don't know what to say. I am so sorry."

"It's OK," I said, trying to hold back the tears. "It's not your fault, Mrs. Golden."

"I'll make it up to you, Freddy. I promise. I'll buy you another pumpkin tomorrow."

"You don't have to do that, Mrs. Golden," said my mom. "But that is very sweet of you to offer."

"Well, there must be something I can do. I feel terrible about this."

"Don't feel bad. Things happen. That's life," said my mom. "We'll just make another one. Come on, Freddy. We've got to go. I almost forgot I have dinner cooking!"

"Good night, Freddy. Good night, Mrs. Thresher. Again, I am so sorry. I'll make it up to you sometime."

As soon as we were far enough away from Mrs. Golden's house, I started to cry. "Now everything's ruined!" I sobbed.

"What are you talking about?" said my mom. "The contest isn't until Friday. I'll get another pumpkin tomorrow, and we'll make a new one."

"But it won't be the same," I said, sniffling.

"What do you mean? We'll make it look just like the one Baxter ate."

"I mean it won't be the pumpkin from the Pumpkin Elf! That was a special pumpkin. I'll never win the contest without the pumpkin from the Pumpkin Elf."

CHAPTER 8

My Lucky Day

The next morning I didn't even want to get out of bed.

"Freddy, let's go! Time to get up!" my mom yelled from downstairs. "It's late!"

I just lay there looking up at the ceiling. Why did this have to happen to me? Why did Baxter have to eat my pumpkin from the Pumpkin Elf? Why couldn't he have eaten a pumpkin from someone else's porch? Why mine? It wasn't fair.

"Freddy!" my mom yelled again. "If you don't get up, you'll miss the bus!"

As if I cared. I didn't even want to go to school. Everyone would be talking about their special pumpkins. Everyone but me.

My dad stuck his head in my room. "Freddy, you really need to get a move on. Breakfast is already on the table."

"All right, Dad. I'm coming," I mumbled.

"I expect you downstairs in five minutes, with your teeth brushed, and your clothes on." He closed the door and left.

I dragged myself out of bed and threw on some clothes. Then I went to the bathroom to brush my teeth. The good thing about getting up late is that I don't have to wait for Princess Suzie to get out of the bathroom.

As I started to walk down the stairs, my mom yelled again, "Freddy, if you're not down here in one minute, you're in big trouble, mister."

I walked into the kitchen just as she finished. "There you are. I thought you were never coming down. What took you so long?"

"I couldn't get out of bed."

"Why not? And why the long face?"

Was she kidding? Did she not remember that last night was one of the worst nights of my whole life?

"Oh, he's just in a bad mood because Baxter ate his stupid pumpkin."

"It was not stupid!" I screamed.

"OK, Freddy, calm down," said my dad. Then he turned to Suzie. "Leave him alone. He's upset."

"I don't know what he's so upset about. Mom said she'd get him another pumpkin."

"But it's not the same!"

"Why not?" asked my dad.

"Because it's not from the Pumpkin Elf."

"A pumpkin's a pumpkin."

"No! The ones from the Pumpkin Elf are special. He grows them with magic seeds."

"He does not," said Suzie.

"Does too!"

"Does not!"

"Enough, you two," said my dad. "I can't believe you are arguing about this. Freddy, I think you need some air. Would you please go out front and bring in the newspaper?"

"Sure, Dad. I'll do anything to get away from Suzie."

"Hurry, honey," my mom called after me.

"The bus will be here soon, and you haven't had a bite of breakfast."

I opened the front door and almost tripped over something on the front porch. I turned around to see what it was, and I almost fainted. I blinked a few times and rubbed my eyes. *This must be a dream*, I thought. There on the porch was a pumpkin decorated exactly like mine. The same mouth, the same gills, the same tail, and the same fin—cut out of the same exact cardboard! I bent down to touch it because I was sure it wasn't real, but it was!

Attached to the pumpkin was a small, orange, pumpkin-shaped note. It said:

Dear Freddy,
I know how upset you were that Baxter
ate your pumpkin, so I made you a new one.
I hope you like it!
Love,
The Pumpkin Elf

"Mom, Dad, Suzie, come quick! Come quick!" I screamed.

They all came running. "What is it, sweetie? Are you all right?" asked my mom.

"The Pumpkin Elf! The Pumpkin Elf!" I yelled, jumping up and down.

"Uh, could you speak English, please?" said Suzie. "I don't know what you're saying."

"The Pumpkin Elf decorated a new pumpkin for me!"

"What?"

"Look at it," I said, holding it up for them all to see. "Isn't it great?"

"It's beautiful. Who made it?"

"The Pumpkin Elf. And he left a note." I handed it to my mom.

"Would you look at that," she said, smiling.

"That was very nice of the Pumpkin Elf," said my dad. "Today's your lucky day!"

"I know it! And tomorrow I am going to win the contest. Thank you, Pumpkin Elf, wherever you are! Thank you, thank you, thank you!"

CHAPTER 9

The Contest

On Friday morning I jumped out of bed. I couldn't wait to get to school. Today was the big day . . . the day of the contest. I was going to win first prize!

When we all got to school, Mrs. Wushy told us to place our pumpkins on the back counter.

"Don't put yours too close to mine," Chloe said to Max. "I don't want the tutu to get ripped." Chloe had decorated hers like a ballerina, of course.

"A tutu?" Max snickered. "Who puts a tutu on a pumpkin? Halloween pumpkins are supposed to look scary like mine." He had made his look like Dracula. It was actually pretty cool, but not as cool as mine.

"I like your pumpkin, Freddy," said Jessie. "It's very original."

"Thanks, Jessie. Where's yours?"

"It's over there. It's the one on the end."

"What did you make?"

"I made the Pumpkin Elf."

"You did? Let me see it." I walked over to where hers was sitting. "That is awesome. What a great idea, Jessie."

"Thanks." She smiled.

"How about you, Robbie? What kind of creature did you make?"

"A bearded dragon."

"A what?"

"It's a lizard that fans out the skin on its neck when it gets scared."

"That's so cool! Is there any animal you don't know about?"

Robbie smiled.

"Okay, everybody, come to the rug," said

Mrs. Wushy. "I have to tell you the rules for the contest. You are all going to be judges."

We sat down. "This is how you are going to judge the pumpkins. Each pumpkin has a number in front of it. Everyone will get a piece of paper like this. You write down the number of the pumpkin that is your favorite. You just can't vote for yourself. Does everybody understand?"

"Yes."

"Great! As soon as I pass out the papers,

then you can get started. Oh! One more thing. There will be no talking while you are judging. I want you to make your own decisions."

There were so many great pumpkins. It was hard to choose. Everybody had really used their imaginations. There was a puppy, a princess, a witch, and a baseball player. (I'm so glad I decided not to do that one.) Suzie's idea was definitely worth doing her chores for two weeks. Mine was definitely the best.

"Try to finish, everyone. Time is almost up," said Mrs. Wushy.

We all hurried.

"Okay, time's up! Give me your papers, and come back to the rug."

Mrs. Wushy put up a big piece of chart paper with everyone's name and pumpkin number. "Each time someone gets a vote, I will put a tally mark next to their name. The person with the most votes will win first place, the runner-up will win second place, and the person with the next most will win third. Let's start."

She went through each paper one at a time and made a tally mark by our name if someone voted for our pumpkin.

When Mrs. Wushy had gotten about halfway through, I was ahead by three votes, with Jessie in second place. "I think you're going to win," Robbie whispered to me.

I smiled. I didn't think. I knew.

Mrs. Wushy continued. When there were

only five votes left to tally, she stopped. "Let's see where we are. It's very close. Freddy has six votes, Jessie has four, Max has three, and Robbie has two."

I was so excited. My heart was pounding so hard I thought it was going to pop out of my chest. I couldn't look. I closed my eyes and waited for it to be over. I waited for Mrs. Wushy to announce my name.

"It was a very close race, boys and girls. One of the closest I've ever had in my class. And this year the winner is . . . "

"Freddy," I whispered under my breath.

"Jessie."

Huh? My eyes flew open. I looked at the chart. Jessie had beaten me by one vote.

"Congratulations, Jessie. You win first prize." She handed Jessie a big trophy and a pumpkin lollipop. "I've never had anyone make their pumpkin into the Pumpkin Elf before. That was a great idea."

"Thank you, Mrs. Wushy," said Jessie. "I worked really hard."

"Freddy, you are our second-place winner and Max, you are third. Would you two boys please come up to get your trophies? Boys and girls, let's give all three of our winners a big round of applause."

Everyone clapped and cheered.

I was a little disappointed that I didn't come in first place. I was so sure I was going to win, but if anyone was going to beat me, I'm glad it was Jessie. She deserves it. Making the Pumpkin Elf really was a great idea.

Besides, I have something that's even better than first place. Something no one else has. A note from the Pumpkin Elf himself!

As I stood at the front of the room listening to my classmates cheer for me, out of the corner of my eye, I thought I saw a little flash of orange . . . could it be?

"Thank you, Pumpkin Elf," I whispered. "Thank you!"

DEAR READER,

I have been a teacher for many years, and every year around Halloween, the Pumpkin Elf pays a visit to my classroom.

The Pumpkin Elf is very small, with a pumpkin-shaped head. He likes to play tricks, but he also leaves treats. We know he's been in the room because he leaves small, orange footprints and pumpkin-shaped clues. When we follow the clues, we always find a surprise—a pumpkin for every child in my class! My students always try to catch the Pumpkin Elf, but he is just too quick.

Have you ever seen the Pumpkin Elf, or do you do something special in your class for Halloween? I'd love to hear about it. Just write to me at:

Ready, Freddy! Fun Stuff
c/o Scholastic Inc.
P. O. Box 711
New York, NY 10013-0711

I hope you have as much fun reading *The Pumpkin Elf Mystery* as I had writing it.

HAPPY READING!

Abby Klein

Freddy's Fun Pages

FREDDY'S SHARK JOURNAL

THE ELECTRIC DETECTIVES

Sharks have rough, sharp skin, and they can feel objects that are nearby, just as you can.

Unlike you, sharks have an organ called the lateral line. This is a long tube that runs down the sides of their bodies—from snout to tail and around each eye—that helps them sense more distant water movement. Very small holes in the skin send signals to the shark's brain.

Sharks have an electrical sense. They have tiny holes around their faces (called *ampullae*) that detect electrical signals from their prey. All animals give off electricity—even you.

Sharks are excellent hunters. Their *ampullae* (AM-pew-lee) allow them to pick up electrical signals, so the sharks know where to find their prey.

MAKE A PUMPKIN ELF BOOKMARK

SUPPLIES:

large wooden craft stick

orange construction paper

colored markers

tape or glue

DIRECTIONS:

1. Color the craft stick in alternating green-and-orange stripes.

2. Draw a pumpkin-shaped head on the orange construction paper, and cut it out.

3. Draw a face on the pumpkin head.

4. Tape or glue the head to the top of the stick.

5. Happy Reading!

PUMPKIN ELF LAUGHTER

Here are some of the Pumpkin Elf's favorite Halloween jokes. Try them on some of your friends!

Q. What is a witch's favorite subject in school?
A. Spelling!

Q. Why didn't the skeleton cross the road?
A. He didn't have the guts!

Q. What does a ghost have for dessert?
A. I-scream!

Q. How do witches keep their hair in place?
A. With Scare Spray.

Q. What do birds give out on Halloween?
A. Tweets.

Q. What kind of dogs do vampires like best?
A. Bloodhounds.

Q. Why do vampires need mouthwash?
A. Because they have bat breath.

Q. What do ghosts put on their cereal?
A. Booberries.

Have you read all about Freddy?

Don't miss any of Freddy's funny adventures!